Death's Secret

Nino Balistreri

balistrerinino338@gmail.com

Historical Fiction

Design: DnA Design House
Cover: DnA Design House

National Library of Canada Cataloguing in Publication
Caruso, Anthony, 1944-
Death's Secret / Nino Balistreri
ISBN: 978-1-7750849-0-7
I. Fiction – History – World War II.

Acknowledgments

Continually for as many years as I can remember, I have been accused of loving to tell stories. At social events they often ran on too long. One day I reached the point of deciding to purge the stories from my head.

I bungled along for a while, before realizing that I needed help. That help was thankfully available at the time. I am now publishing, thanks to the lessons and guidance acquired from working with E Alex Pierce, an award winning Canadian poet. Alex with the financial support and encouragement from the Shelburne County Arts Council helped to launch me in the right direction.

It has also been a wonderful experience to work for two winters in Florida, with the 'Pine Island Writers' group. In our weekly meetings, they provide the sounding board that is much needed to keep my story lines real and focused.

The article “German U-Boat Surrenders” is based on one in the Coast Guard Newspaper circa May 20, 1945.

Finally I would like to thank Darcy Rhyno and Alex Buchanan - DnA Design House – for their help in design, layout and formatting of this book.

1. News From Afar

Reporter Jeff Hendricks sat in the breakfast room, of an old East Coast Inn. The Halifax news had rushed him to the picturesque seaside town of Shelburne.

His editor had few details to give him. For the last few days he had been picking up snippets of rumors, via the news services.

It was evident that something big was happening down the shore. From questions in fishing for details, he deducted that it had something to do with the Second World War and lost secrets.

The final clincher was a call that he received from an old colleague, who now was editor of the local newspaper. His friend Wilson was not happy about the situation. He took a risk in calling his colleague Fred in Halifax to try and skirt around the authorities. "Hi Fred, Wilson calling from down the shore. I am being strangled with an official government gag order. Things are happening and my hands are tied. I am so mad."

"After all of these years stagnating here, I finally have the scoop of a lifetime and I can't publish, by order of National Defense."

"This story is going to blow soon. The locals are wise to it. I know that it is just a matter of time before it runs away in spite of the military. The rumors from across the harbour are too wild. But if they are true, heads will roll in the national security service."

"I have to get off this line before someone overhears me. Just get a good reporter here fast. You didn't hear it from me. He needs to look up a Laurel and Dale Peters. I am not allowed to interview them. But if your guy can sneak in unnoticed, he can get an exclusive."

"They are staying at the old Inn across from my offices. That is all I can give you and keep out of jail."

Fred had received a lot of news tips over the years. This one definitely was the strangest. All hints and no real details.

Jeff was just starting to sip his coffee when a rather pale and nervous looking Laurel and Dale joined him, in the Inn's breakfast room.

Jeff had called ahead and made the initial contact. He hoped that his call had not been forwarded to the authorities.

Once introductions were done and more coffee served, Laurel began to relate their story.

Before she could say a lot, they were interrupted by a Naval Captain and an RCMP Officer. The Naval Captain wasted no time in informing Jeff, "You may not proceed with this interview. Homeland Security has an order in place to disallow any recording or reporting of this situation."

Jeff countered, "From what I have heard, everyone in the area knows what is happening. If you won't allow me to interview these people, I will just fish around and piece it together on my own."

Looking to the RCMP officer, The Naval Captain nodded. They both knew when they were beat.

Turning to Jeff he announced, "I don't know how you got this far, or how you found the Peters name. But you are here and already know too much. I could arrest you for trying to breach the order. But I won't. We have enough to deal with."

"What I will do is allow you to conduct this interview. Providing you sign a sworn affidavit that you will not release or publish a word. Not until clearance is given by

National Defense in Ottawa. If you breach this agreement, then I will have no hesitation in ordering your arrest."

Jeff knew when he was in a corner. He needed a good scoop. His reporting career was stagnant.

"I agree to your terms. I will swear an oath under one condition. I must be the only interview, before this goes public. It must be an exclusive."

Both the RCMP and Naval Captain agreed. They looked over their shoulder and nodded. No one at the table had noticed the four burly shore patrol officers. They were standing at ease in the Inn's lobby. They parted and a regular navy corporal stepped forward. He was carrying a steno pad and a bible.

A statement was dictated and duly sworn and signed by all parties. Once this was complete, Jeff thought that the military would leave. Instead they dismissed the shore patrol and stenographer. Then pulled up chairs.

The RCMP told Jeff, "We will sit in on the interview to make sure that no further laws are breached."

Jeff was not happy about this new development, but had no choice. He got out his hand recorder and asked Laurel, "Would you kindly begin again so that I can record the information.

Now totally frazzled, Laurel began her tale.

"Back in June, we received a letter from a lawyer in this town. It announced that Dale's uncle Albert had died. In his will he left Dale a property on the harbour. It's a parcel of several acres, in a place called Fort Point."

"The letter went on to state, that there was a little over five hundred dollars owed, in back taxes. To complete the terms of Uncle Albert's will, the house was to be bulldozed and the basement filled in."

"The estimated cost of this would be fifteen hundred dollars."

Laurel went on, "We read the letter over several times. Dale and I both agreed on what we believed to be the best decision. We scheduled a trip east for our summer vacation. At the time we didn't know where Shelburne was, other than the fact that it was on the east coast."

Dale broke in, "I went on line and found it on Google Maps. Seeing where it was located, I remembered that one of my fellow teachers had talked about being from this area. The following day I approached him in the teachers lounge."

"He recommended a place to stay, so that we could make reservations. He urged that we do it fast. It will be hi season, when we arrived. He also gave us his father's contact information, for local directions."

Laurel added, "That evening we sent an Email to the lawyer. We confirmed that we would pay the back taxes, but did not want the house bulldozed until we arrived to inspect it."

Laurel could tell that Jeff looked confused. All this official carrying on, over the inheritance of a property, made no sense.

She helped re gain his interest by stating, "It is hard to believe all that has happened to us in just a few short weeks."

"After logging off that evening, I realized that Dale was sitting quietly in his chair. He had a 'far away' look on his face. He seemed unaware at first that I was even in the room. I had to ask twice, why he had never mentioned having an Uncle Albert?"

"After what seemed forever, Dale cued in and finally answered me. It was as if he was talking from a distant world, or time."

"He told me that the last time he had thought about

Uncle Albert, was when his own dad died."

Hearing this, Dale picked up the story, "A few days after dad's funeral, I went to the bank and emptied his safety deposit box. I took the contents to my mother. She had not wanted to deal with this alone."

"There was the usual array of papers. The house deed and three insurance policies. At the bottom of the pile I found an old yellowed envelope."

"I opened it and read it to my mother. The letter was to my dad from Uncle Albert. The contents were puzzling. It made no sense to me at the time."

"I had no sooner read the last distressing words. When my mother approached me. She snatched the letter from my hands, rushed across the room and flung it into the burning fireplace."

"When she turned to face me, I just sat there in shock. Before my eyes my mother had been transformed into a tortured looking woman."

"She was like a total stranger to me. She spoke in a cruel hard tone. One that I had never heard her use, in my entire life."

"How dare he! Your father gave me his word. That letter was to be destroyed years ago. He had no right to place us all in danger, by keeping it. If you love me, you will forget that you ever saw it."

"Mother then clammed up completely. I never found out any more, about the reason behind that letter. I just wish that she was still alive. I could talk to her about the amazing things that we discovered."

"She was obviously aware of Uncle Albert's political beliefs. I can only wonder if she knew what he was actually hiding."

"Given the time and circumstances, mom was certainly justified in fearing danger for our entire family."

"I am sure that Mom, Dad and Uncle Albert would have at least been imprisoned. Or worse still, executed as traitors. Either way I would have been left an orphan in care. We had no other family."

At this point, Jeff Hendricks broke in, "If you only read that letter once, years ago, before your mother destroyed it. How can you actually remember it in such detail?"

In answer to this Laurel reached into her handbag. She placed on the table, a file folder of papers. Opening it up she spread the items around for all to see.

There was Uncle Albert's will and the deed to his property at Fort Point. Also a statement from the funeral service that handled his cremation, plus the lawyers' bill.

From amongst it all, Laurel drew out an old yellowed document. Carefully unfolding it, she handed it to Jeff.

It was a carbon copy, of the hated letter that Uncle Albert had sent to Dale's father. Like the one that Dale had read years before, it was in Uncle Albert's own handwriting.

Dear Fredrick

I know that you no longer wish to hear from me, but I had to write. I am sorry that we are so different in views and political beliefs. It has caused us to be strangers. I now realize that you were right. No penance can make up for the wrong that I have done. It is a burden that will weigh me for the rest of my life. My only peace is in the knowledge that it is finally over. It has been laid to rest. My soul shall forever burn in the depths of what I have created. I have no right to ask you and Martha for forgiveness. I will only ask that some day, you will be able to reach out to me. It weighs heavy on my heart that we may end our days as strangers.

Always your brother, Albert

2. The Arrival

From the moment that the lawyers' letter arrived and the final days of teaching approached. Dale became more and more apprehensive. He could not shake off the sense of foreboding.

Perhaps this trip was not a good idea. He discussed it with Laurel. She was excited about the adventure. He finally agreed to go east as planned. He hoped that they would find the answer to this puzzle.

Dale had only three weeks off. He had an important course to attend. The day after school ended, they headed east. All through the drive, not a mention was made of the letter that Dale's mother had burned. Or what they might find, on arrival at the coast.

Both were plagued with an uneasy feeling, about the meaning that lurked behind it. Was uncle Albert a criminal, or some kind of horrible person?

Dale had a vague memory, of a trip to the east coast. But it was back when he was probably no older than eight or ten.

He had no actual memories of Uncle Albert. Had he suppressed something traumatic? Or was the visit too brief, to leave a lasting impression on a young child?

Arriving in Shelburne, Dale and Laurel checked into the old Inn. Once settled, Dale called his colleagues father. Within an hour, he met them for coffee.

Mr. Burns was a pleasant courteous man, with a welcoming personality. He gave them directions to the lawyers' office, as well as to the property at Fort Point.

The following morning, Laurel and Dale met with the lawyer. They took care of the legal end of paying the back taxes and transferring ownership.

They also learned that uncle Albert had lived for many years at Fort Point. He was locally known as a recluse. He did not associate closely with neighbors or townspeople. He had spent the last six years of his life in a local long term care home.

Albert had refused to rent out or sell the property. They were informed that the house had sadly fallen into severe neglect. The lawyer was certain that the house was in no way habitable. This dampened Laurel and Dale's hopes of a summer home by the sea.

That evening over a meal of fresh seafood, Laurel the eternal optimist, convinced herself that the house would indeed be sound and salvageable.

Dale tried to not encourage Laurel's train of thought, for fear that she will end up too disappointed. But at the same time, he was harboring similar fantasies.

The letter and the mystery surrounding it, still clung to the back of their minds. Dale didn't sleep well that night. He kept dreaming about his mother, even though the event happened many years ago at the time of his dads' death.

He could still visualize the look of terror and hatred on her face. The day that she turned on him was totally clear today, as if it happened just last week.

The next morning was foggy. Their waitress Debby assured them that the sun would shortly burn through.

True to her word, Two hours later, Dale and Laurel were driving the shore route out of Shelburne. It wound through Birchtown, Churchover, Gunning Cove and finally there it was.

A highway sign pointing off to the left marked Fort Point. Leaving the pavement behind they drove towards the harbour, down a narrow gravel road. It meandered past an old farmstead and several treed driveways. All were marked with numbered mailboxes, some also containing family names. Each one was mounted on a low standing post.

Finally they reached the end of the road. As directed, Dale turned towards an overgrown lane. It displayed a No Trespassing sign.

It was suspended from a rusted chain that spanned the driveway entrance. The chain was affixed to posts. The left one had faded numbers nailed to it. The remnants of a rusted mailbox sat atop the left post.

3. Disappointment

Dale stepped out of the car. He found that the chain was not locked, just hooked in place. Climbing back behind the wheel, they proceeded to slowly drive down the curved lane. It was badly overgrown, with tall grasses and weeds.

It meandered past an old barn that looked to be quite sound.

Then past a garage that had no door. This building was leaning at a near collapsing angle.

Coming to a halt, they sat in the car for a few minutes. Both were trying to absorb the sight that lay before them. The little one and a half story house, was indeed in a sad state. It had broken windows and a general look of decay.

Finally Dale gathered up enough nerve to exit the car. Carefully winding his way through the tall weeds. He slowly approached the house, with Laurel following close behind. Reaching it, they stepped gingerly onto a small stoop.

It was a pleasant enough looking salt box style of old house.

Yet as Dale lifted the rusted latch and eased the creaking door slowly open, chills ran up and down his spine.

Once it was swung wide, Dale turned to Laurel. The look on her face mirrored the feeling in his stomach. Dale grasped Laurel's hand. Together they stepped into the living room.

There was not much in this room. The floor had a layer of worn oilcloth. Two old sofa chairs, leaking stuffing. Two small tables, one tipped over with a broken leg. The wallpaper was stained and yellowed. The curtains had fallen to the floor in shreds.

The main floor consisted of two other rooms. A large farm style kitchen, containing a hand pump and an old Key Mack stove. Beside it mounted on the wall, there was a small oil barrel and under that a wooden box. It contained pieces of split firewood.

Obviously Uncle Albert had used the duel fuel stove, to cook with and heat the house. The kitchen also contained an assortment of worn out and broken furniture and utensils.

Off the kitchen was a smaller room, obviously Uncle Albert's bedroom. It had wall hooks, hung with old clothes. Also a single cot and a small table. This was piled with tattered newspapers and magazines.

A search of the upstairs two rooms did not reveal a great deal more. Lots of old newspapers and general trash. A few pieces of broken furniture, an old iron bedstead.

This was thankfully devoid of a mattress.

Back on the main floor, they walked silently out the kitchen door. It was located on the opposite side of the house. Dale and Laurel sat on the edge of another small stoop. They were feeling totally overwhelmed and exhausted.

After what seemed a long while, their eyes began to focus on the incredible vista of the harbour.

4. The Harbour

It took a small fishing boat steaming past, to break their spell. They had only to look to the right, to see past the mouth of the harbour, to the open ocean. This vantage point afforded them an unobstructed view, of anything that came or went by water.

As their eyes followed the fishing boat, towards the Gunning Cove wharf, they were awed by the pristine beauty of the harbour. The elevation of their spot on Fort Point also afforded a panoramic view of the ship yards, fish plants and the town.

Directly across the harbour and slightly to the left, sat a beautiful old lighthouse. It seemed in an odd place, sitting surrounded by relatively calm, deep water. The reason for its positioning was evident the following day. At low tide, a sand bar curved out from the shore, to the base of the lighthouse.

This effectively created a barrier across a good one third of the harbour entrance.

They later found out that it was appropriately called

'The Sandy Point Light'. The sand bar and light forced all marine traffic to steam closer to the Fort Point side of the harbour entrance.

After sitting a while, Laurel and Dale decided to explore the property. The going was difficult. It was wildly grown in with thickets of raspberry and alders.

Remnants of a path wound down the embankment towards the shore. It was not as heavily grown in, suggesting that it had been in more recent use.

At the bottom of the path, emerging from the tall grasses and brush, they were rewarded to find a small sand beach.

It was surrounded by large rocks, with the remnants of an old boat haul-up. It sat like a little secret pocket, all tucked in and protected.

Dale felt the water. He was pleasantly surprised. It was no cooler than the lake water back home. He sat on a rock, removed his runners and socks and rolled up his jean legs. It did not take much wading to see that the water was clear. The bottom had a gradual sandy slope.

Wading back up onto the beach, Dale started to strip.

Laurel being more modest began to laugh telling Dale, "You do realize, there is probably a law out here against public nudity."

Stripped, Dale stuck his tongue out at Laurel. He then ran and dove into the harbour. The water was refreshing. He swam back and forth below the house, exploring the rocks and shoreline.

He tried several times to coax Laurel into joining him. Laurel just laughed claiming, "Someone has to be dressed to bail you out, when you are arrested for public nudity." Dale wished that he had his fins and mask. He made a mental note to bring them, on his next trip from town.

Swimming back towards the beach for the last time, Dale dove underwater. He wanted to try and determine how far down the bottom was.

He descended as deep as he could, fighting the natural buoyancy of the salt water.

As he swam underwater, parallel to the shore, the toes of his right foot connected painfully with something solid.

Startled, Dale surfaced and felt his foot, to determine if it was cut. While doing this, he drifted slightly with the current. He soon realized that he was resting his left foot on a smooth level surface.

Back paddling a bit, Dale discovered the probable cause of his pain.

The smooth surface jutted out from the uneven rock face, for about three feet, then dropped off with a sharp edge. It was covered with a fine coating of green sea growth.

This hid the fact that it was manmade concrete, rather than a natural rock formation.

Now surfaced, Dale swam back to the beach. As he walked to the rock where his clothes were resting, Laurel noticed him limping. When he explained what had happened, she scolded, "It serves you right. You know better than to freely swim in strange waters."

As the afternoon was getting on, they had absorbed just about enough for one day. It was time to head back to the Inn, to get cleaned up for supper.

5. Plans

That night both Laurel and Dale lay awake for a long time. Thinking about the house, the property and the incredible harbour view. The following morning at breakfast, Dale got up the nerve to broach the subject. “You know dear, I have been thinking about Fort Point.”

Laurel began to laugh, “It took you long enough to decide. I made up my mind yesterday, that we should keep the house.”

Over two china pots of coffee, they made plans, to clean out the house and make it weather tight. Beyond that the second goal was to collect enough necessities to camp in it for the summer, like a wooden tent. This would allow them enough time to clear the brush and make plans for next summer’s restoration work.

Laurel being a 'Do it now' person decided, “If we gather enough basic supplies, I can stay behind to get a head start on the work. You can fly home alone for your two week certification course.”

They spent the morning shopping for brooms, mops, buckets, shovels and basic tools. Plus a good supply of cleaning chemicals, rags and paper products.

They also needed to locate the county dump and the hours of operation. Dale was not comfortable with burning the paper and wood refuse. At least not until the property was safely cleared.

Taking their purchases out to Fort Point, the next chore was to measure up the missing panes of glass. The local hardware could pre cut them. Dale scrambled around the exterior with a measuring tape, as Laurel listed the location and sizes.

Later after an early supper, Laurel and Dale drove back out to Fort Point. They sat on the rocks by the beach, to watch the fishing boats come and go. At one point a Coast guard cutter left the harbour.

It soon returned with a small fishing boat under tow. Then a pair of sleek yachts sailed in. They were obviously traveling together.

The following morning at breakfast, the innkeeper told them, "Many famous yachts and personalities visit this harbour. They come in to clear customs for

Canadian waters, or to shelter from North Atlantic hurricanes and gales.

They watched the sunset behind them, as it reflected vivid colors on the water. It was soon time to head back to the inn. Both Laurel and Dale realized that taking advantage of the lengthy daylight and twilight would not provide enough illumination.

They would need to add a couple of lanterns and torches to the shopping list. The pick-nick cooler from home would do for now. They would also need a camp stove and a few pots and utensils.

It seemed strange to have to purchase pots, dishes and utensils, when this had been a home for many years. Had it all been given away? Or worse, had the house been looted, after uncle Albert moved to the seniors residence?

6. Work Starts

Early the next morning, dressed in jeans and T shirts, they quickly ate breakfast. Dale was anxious about starting the work on the house.

He still expressed to Laurel, “deep inside, I still have an eerie feeling about this whole situation.”

Laurel assured Dale that it was foolish to feel this way, “I am sure that your uneasiness is just excitement.”

Had Dale known what lay ahead, he might have complied with his uncle's will, to have the house bulldozed and the basement filled in. Or would he?

Leaving the Inn, they first stopped at the hardware, to pick up the glass order. Also a supply of putty, points and more small tools.

Dale priced shingles for the worn out house roof. After having the process of stripping, re sheeting and shingling explained, they made a decision that it would be beyond their abilities.

A proper roofing contractor would have to be hired to do the job. The builders’ desk gave Dale several cards from local roofers that do business with them.

Arriving at the house, Dale started to repair the broken windows. They were mostly on the ground floor. He found an old split pole ladder in the barn. It was solid enough to use.

Laurel started on the second floor with garbage bags, sifting through the clutter. At lunch break Laurel told Dale, "I found little of interest and nothing worth saving."

"I just can't understand this situation. This house had been lived in for so many years. Yet it is totally devoid of personal belongings and memorabilia. You inherited your father's trait for being a first class pack rat. It is unreal that your uncle's house should be so barren of personal belongings."

Just as they were finishing lunch, perched on the edge of the stoop, a sudden commotion erupted from the driveway. It was in the form of a black and white spaniel.

He was growling and barking, with the attitude that they did not belong there. A minute later a young teenage boy and girl followed, running around the corner.

The boy was a tall husky teenager, with short fair hair. His younger sister was quite the opposite. She was short and extremely petite, with shoulder length light brown hair, tied back by a bright yellow ribbon.

The brother was clad in cut off jeans and a rock group T shirt. He was sporting fluorescent colored sneakers, devoid of socks.

The girl was wearing a colorful printed bright green top, with pink pedal pushers. Her sneakers were sunshine yellow.

Laurel smiled when she took in the girls outfit. When she was ten, much to the chagrin of her mother, she wore similar multicolored combinations. On the days that Laurel decided to wear her favorite colors, she turned a deaf ear to her mother's preaching and disregarded all laws of coordination.

Lauren decided that these two must have free spirited parents. Loving adults, who allowed their children to openly express their personalities.

In unison, both children were quick to quiet the spaniel, whose name was Colby.

They then introduced themselves. The elder was Sol and his sister Kaela. They lived in the first farm house, at the top of the road.

Sol admitted, "We have been watching you drive by

every day." There was evidently no shyness displayed here.

Kaela wanted to know, "Do you have any kids? They can ride the school bus with us. Will you be moving in here?"

Laurel answered, "No" to both questions. She told them, "Dale will be leaving in a week or so. Then he will return for the balance of the summer. We have a lot of clearing and cleaning to do, even before we start to seriously repair and renovate the house."

Sol quickly suggested, "If you need help, I could use a summer job. I cut the lawns for several of our neighbors. My dad pays me an allowance to cut our lawn. I am a hard worker and strong for my age. But I can't get a real paying summer job for another year and a half, when I turn sixteen."

Kaela immediately piped in, "Me too, I need a job. I can help Sol." Both Laurel and Dale were delighted with the youngsters' enthusiasm.

Laurel replied, "If it is OK with your parents, we will gratefully accept your offer. Help of all kinds is certainly needed around here."

Kaela and Sol confessed, "We often swim off Mr.

Albert's beach, but only with our parents."

"We are not allowed near the water alone. Mr. Albert always let us to swim here, as long as we promised to never bring other people. He liked our mom and dad. They let him use our phone to call in his food order every month. Mom always brought him some baking and food. She said that Albert was not a good cook."

Laurel assured them that they could continue to swim from the little beach. This explained the worn path that led from the driveway to the beach.

Laurel and Dale spent the balance of the day completing the tasks at hand. Dale finished installing the panes of glass, and Laurel completed clearing the rooms upstairs.

In the smaller of the two rooms, there was a hatchway, built into the knee wall. It opened to a storage space in the west eave. The door was nailed shut. It took a pry bar to open it.

Laurel visualized it holding many treasures. She was disappointed to find only a broken bed head board and two broken chairs.

As the afternoon ended, Laurel and Dale decided not to

make it a marathon, on the first day. There was just too much to do.

7. New Friends

Thanking Kaela and Sol for their offer to help, Laurel and Dale prepared to head back to town. At the top of the road they stopped at the kids' home. Their mother Kim was a happy lady who welcomed them to the neighborhood. There were no explanations to give.

Kaela and Sol had already burst into the house, telling their mom all the news about the new neighbors. Kim was more than happy to let the kids hang out and help in any way.

She admitted, "There is not a lot to entertain the kids here in the summer. They love being near the water. It will keep them busy, having time to help you with your projects."

Leaving there, Laurel and Dale headed back to town. They grabbed an early supper at the seafood takeout, and then got cleaned up.

A notice posted in the Inn's lobby announced that the local Historical Society was meeting that evening. Perhaps there would be someone there who knew Uncle

Albert?

The meeting was held in a historic waterfront building. As well as the meeting room, it housed a large craft center. In there, the local guild worked on hooked rugs and quilts.

After a gracious introduction, the president of the society requested, “If anyone here has knowledge of Albert Peters who lived at Fort Point, would you please come forward during the social?”

That evening, their mystery only deepened. Several people came forward and stated that they had known Albert for many years. But they knew little about him personally. Everyone admitted that Albert was a recluse. He paid his bills and as far as they knew, lived frugally. It was unanimous that although he was often aloof, he was polite in any business dealings.

A Mrs. Lang suggested they talk to her sister, who runs the old family grocery business. She was quite certain that Albert had dealt with them.

The following morning they combined the need for lunch supplies, with a visit to Grovestine's Grocery. The proprietor Mary Lou, was quite helpful.

Uncle Albert had indeed dealt with them for many

years. He was remembered as a polite and quiet gentleman.

Mary Lou was able to tell Laurel and Dale just a little more about their uncle. "Albert called in his weekly or at times monthly order.

"He did not have a phone, so had to use a neighbors. We always delivered to him on the day that boat orders were run around the harbour, to Gunning Cove."

Mary Lou added, "From what we were able to observe, Albert had little and lived without any comforts."

"We were all relieved when Albert moved to the seniors residence. He was at least kept warm and well fed there."

"Twice in his last year at Fort Point, my brother convinced Albert to ride back to town with him. He needed to see the doctor; he looked so weak and poorly." Laurel thanked Mary Lou for her help and information.

Walking back to the Inn, Laurel gave Dale a hug. He asked, "What was that for?" Laurel told him, "I am just feeling good. It is heartwarming to know that our waitress Debby is right. Mary Lou does care for and adopts all those around her who are in need. Now we know why everyone we talk to, refers to her as 'Mamma Lou'."

Both Laurel and dale had a good feeling inside. Knowing that there was still a place in this hectic world, where people took time to care.

8. Puzzling Discovery

The plan that day, was to start the main floor cleanup. The sun pouring into the living room, prompted Laurel and Dale to start there.

They worked from the top down, sweeping the cobwebs from the ceiling and walls. Then taking down and bagging what was left of the old curtains and sorting through the debris on the floor.

Kaela and Sol arrived mid morning to pitch in. Colby was not with the kids today. When Laurel asked about him, Kaela stated, "He runs off most mornings and walks the miles to town, to visit all of his good friends. I think that their owners also feed him every day, because he is too fat."

Once the living room was cleared and swept, it was evident that the oilcloth had to go. The finish was completely worn off, except for the back two corners. Laurel assured Dale that it would be impossible to keep clean.

Peering under one corner, dale could see that the floor

was built out of wide wood plank boards.

Encouraged by this, he started to rip up the oilcloth, stuffing it into garbage bags. The task was nearly complete, when Dale sensed something.

He straightened up and looked across the room. Laurel was standing off to one side, near the kitchen door. She had a look of fear and terror on her face.

Dale asked her, "What is wrong? Are you OK?" Laurel was unable to answer him. She just pointed to the center of the floor. Together they slowly approached and looked down. Neither wanting to touch it, for fear of what it contained. An old yellowed envelope was heavily taped to the floor. It left no doubt that it had been placed there intentionally.

Crouching down to examine it closer, Dale knew for sure then. His feelings of foreboding were real, not a figment of his imagination. He slowly peeled the envelope from the floor. The tape had little adhesive left. It was quite brittle.

Kaela and Sol were now beside them, drawn into the drama of the moment. With a rapidly beating heart, Dale slowly opened the envelope. It contained several yellowed newspaper clippings. They all sat on the floor, while Laurel read them aloud.

German U-Boat Surrenders

As the White Ensign fluttered to the flagstaff atop German U-Boat no. 889 at 3:24 pm ADT Sunday afternoon, The Royal Canadian Navy took formal possession of the first Nazi underwater craft surrendering to the Canadian Forces since the German capitulation in Europe.

The formal surrender was carried out about eight miles off this base, as Captain ER Miles, RCN Chief of Staff to the Commander-in-Chief of the Canadian Northwest Atlantic, accepted the vessel from the German Commander.

Eight vessels stood by during the ceremony, five of them from Shelburne.

The Canadian Frigate HMCS Buckingham and HMCS Inch Aaron which conveyed the U-Boat from the point which she surrendered, in the North Atlantic, off Newfoundland, stood by the historic ceremony and RCAF aircraft droned overhead.

It was an RCAF Liberator, stationed in Newfoundland which stood guard over the U-Boat in the Atlantic, until the Canadian Frigates showed up, to take her in tow. Other RCAF aircraft circled overhead, during the voyage to this port, for the surrender.

A Royal Navy submarine crew is reported en route, to take command of the German vessel, and the Nazi crew were brought ashore at this base for questioning.

Dressed in Grey Naval uniforms, the U-Boat crew looked young and inexperienced.

The U-Boat wearing dark grey war paint, was about 750 tonnes burden, and carried a crew of between 50 and 60.

She was armed with twin Bofors, quick firing guns, on the platform aft of the conning tower. While she carried light anti aircraft weapons on the conning tower itself. She had no long range rifle on the foredeck, unlike so many of the undersea raiders, who proved themselves more than a match, for merchant seamen, and light naval craft, in wartime surface duels.

On the starboard, or right hand side of the conning tower was the German snorkel apparatus, an ingenious device perfected by the Germans late in the war, so the U-Boats could refill their air tanks without coming to the surface, and meeting possible danger.

Small Canadian Naval craft Bearing official, and press representatives chugged out from the base to meet the incoming German raider, and watch the formal surrender.

After that, she and her crew were brought in here, and taken in charge by personnel of the base, commanded by Captain Colin Donald RCN. This was the first German U-Boat surrendering in North American waters. The U-889 left Norway on April 5th. It was off the Grand Banks of Newfoundland, when Admiral Carl Doenitz broadcast the surrender to all undersea craft.

According to the captain of the craft, "(Kervetten CAP. LT. CMDR) Frederich Breucer, 26 year old native of Hamburg, the U-Boat was headed for New York, to attack shipping, at the head of the harbour. When the signal was received, the U-Boat immediately surfaced and began signaling its position, the German Captain told interpreters. A liberator from the RCAF station at Gander Newfoundland sighted the U-Boat at 3 pm ADT May 10th.

The Canadian Corvette HMCS Rockliffe, took over two hours after the U-Boat was first sighted, and 24 hours later Buckingham and Inch Aaron steamed up, to take over the chore. No boarding party was put on the sub, because of rough seas, so she was escorted in with her original crew at the controls. She was due to arrive off this port at 7 Sunday morning, but bad weather, and poor visibility slowed up the U-Boat and her convoy escorts.

The oldest member of the crew was 33, and the youngest 19, most of the others being in their early twenties. The U-Boat Captain who wore the Iron Cross Second Class and Destroyer Insignia, had been a professional seaman eight years, he said. He claimed that he had never sunk a ship while in command of the U889, and in fact never had a battle contact. When the craft left Norway last month, the crew had no idea the war would be over so quickly, he asserted. "I would like to stay in Canada, or the United States after the war," he told an interpreter. "Germany as a political interest is dead." Asked if he could live in The United States and accept democracy, the U-Boat captain shrugged and answered, "There is not such a big difference between your government and ours."

Laurel paused, as if staring at the article would give her a reason for it all. Realizing that Kaela, Sol and Dale were staring at her, she slowly started to read the second article.

U-889 Lost

It was officially announced today the U-889, the first U-Boat surrendering to Canadian authorities, after being De-ammunitioned left Shelburne Harbour 7:00 am May 20 commanded by a Royal Navy prize crew.

They officially took charge of the craft, after the German Crew were removed. The U-Boat was scheduled to be motored to New York for study, and eventual dismantling. She was escorted to the mouth of Shelburne Harbour, by several local fishing craft and one Coast Guard Cutter.

Once clear of the harbour mouth due to high seas, she submerged for her passage to New York. In his statement to the press, Captain Colin Donald RCN confirmed, that there would be an investigation into the loss. Local views are that, as the prize crew were not trained for U-Boats, they would have been at a disadvantage if any crisis arose.

9. Questions

It made no sense. Why would Uncle Albert go through so much trouble, to hide newspaper articles? They were public property! It was just one more piece added to the puzzle, of ever mounting secrets.

Once finished up in the living room, they started to repeat the process in the small bedroom, off the kitchen. Laurel and dale were relieved to find that this room held no surprises.

Sunlight was still streaming in. They decided to tackle the kitchen. Like all the other rooms, the kitchen was sparsely fitted out. It was hard to believe that it had been lived in and used.

By the time the kitchen was cleared, Laurel and Dale were physically and emotionally exhausted. Ripping up the oilcloth could wait till tomorrow.

It was unanimous. A swim to end the work day was in order. Now that there was young members on their team, Dale made sure to have his bathing suit, and towels handy at all times.

That evening back at the Inn, they read the articles once more. But were still unable to understand why Uncle Albert hid them.

Dale was quite positive that neither his dad nor Uncle Albert had served in the military. He could envision no obvious connection.

That night they slept well, thanks to the fresh air and physical labor. Had either Laurel or Dale suspected what discoveries lay ahead, they certainly would not have slept at all.

The next morning after breakfast, Laurel and Dale went across the street to The Genealogical Society office. They figured that it would be the best place to inquire about the U-889. Laurel took the newspaper articles with them, for reference.

The lady on duty that morning actually knew someone who had been on board the U-Boat, as a 12 year old child. She related, "It happened just before the prize crew arrived to motor the U-Boat out of Shelburne Harbour. The townspeople were allowed to go aboard."

"Most of the town's children could only clearly remember their times, as military and war life. All were ecstatic at being allowed to go aboard an enemy U-Boat."

After an interesting discussion, they left the Genealogical Society. Dale and Laurel drove out to Fort Point and started to work.

The first task of the day was to load the bags of garbage and the two old overstuffed chairs for transport to the dump.

The next chore was to rip up the oilcloth from the kitchen floor. All went well at first. Laurel began to clean the dirt coated kitchen windows, while Dale began the process of stripping the floor.

Just as he stared to fill the first bag, Kaela and Sol arrived. Sol pitched in to help Dale and Kaela took to helping Laurel.

As Dale passed the three quarters point on the floor, a strip of oilcloth that came away revealed a framed corner piece. It was set flush into the floor boards.

The expression on Dale's face mirrored Laurel's. Both sensed that they were about to experience, yet another episode of mystery.

10. Hidden Below

Once the oilcloth was cleared and bagged, all four stood looking at a large trap door. It was hinged on the wall side. On close inspection, Dale could see that it was heavily nailed shut.

Laurel suggested, “It does not really have to be opened.”

Dale agreed, “True but I feel that having gone this far and not knowing what is down there would be worse.” His logic was certainly off this time!

Dale slowly worked his way around the edges of the door, using his pry bar. The wood being so old splintered everywhere he applied pressure.

Finally the door was free. Dale cautiously lifted it to the open position, resting it against the wall. They all solemnly gazed into a black void. A quick trip to the car produced two lanterns and a flashlight.

Now was the moment of truth, as the flashlight beam shone into the void.

The first shock was to see what looked like a solid

stairway. It led down about eight feet to a cement floor.

Everything else in the house was so old and decrepit, it made no sense. Dale tested the first step with one foot, it held. Placing both feet and his entire weigh on it, he realized that it was indeed solid. With the narrow beam of the flashlight lighting his way, he slowly started down the stairs. Laurel grabbed his free hand and followed with Kaela and Sol in tow.

Dale had many times heard or read the phrase, 'My heart was pounding with terror'. This was the first time in his life, that he could truly relate to it.

The glow of the flashlight did little to ease their apprehension. The four explorers descended the stairs, to the unknown.

As his eyes adjusted to the dark, Dale slowly swung the beam around, to survey their surroundings. The fear of what might lay ahead, bristled up his spine.

It came as quite a shock, when Dale realized that he had rotated completely around. Being in such a state, he could not comprehend what he had seen.

All four retreated back up to the kitchen. They stood there for what seemed an eternity, but was in fact, just a couple of minutes. Laurel's only word was a weak,

"Well". Dale swallowed shaking his head.

He decided that both lanterns would be needed to light the entire basement.

He lit the lanterns, then returned down the stairs. Dale found several hooks that were mounted on the ceiling beams. Using these, he hung the lanterns on either side of the staircase. Satisfied that they were secure, Dale took a deep breath and turned to face Laurel.

Kaela and Sol had stopped three quarters of the way down. They immediately rushed towards them. Fear was raging in all their veins. Had Laurel touched Dale, she would have felt his entire being shaking.

For the first time, Laurel and dale started to move around the basement.

They were trying to both grasp and analyze what they were seeing. It seemed too simple.

In one corner, a small pile of kindling. In another, two apple crates filled with empty canning jars. In a third corner stood a small work bench. It had hand tools neatly arranged. They were hanging from rough planks that were mounted to the wall.

The only other thing in the basement was a shelving unit. This was located against the center of the wall, immediately opposite the base of the staircase. This was also built with rough boards. The shelves held some odd bits of junk and an assortment of old jars of preserves. They had long ago lost their color.

Everything was covered with a film of dust, which was obviously many years in gathering. Dale could not realize what was staring him in the face. It was Laurel who finally stated, “Neat, I mean neat and tidy.” She was right as usual. After the mess of the house, they found the basement to be unnaturally neat and organized.

The foundation was made of field stone, as expected for a house of that age. But strangely it had been carefully mortared in with cement. The floor, instead of being the expected dirt, had been smoothly cemented.

Why would it be so finished and organized, after the condition of the house above? A costly cement floor made no sense.

11. Plans Changed

Once again emotionally drained, they climbed the staircase, back to the kitchen. Kaela and Sol left for home. Dale and Laurel decided to have a swim and then call it a day. Any further exploring could wait for another day.

Never had either of them anticipated so much mystery and tension, in just clearing out an old abandoned house. On the way to town they detoured, in order to unload the refuse at the county dump.

Back at the Inn, it was time to clean up and get something to eat. Laurel and Dale spent the evening wandering the waterfront streets. It was a pleasant and relaxing relief, to walk around looking at the old Loyalist homes.

Along the historic waterfront, they came upon Mrs. Benson, from the Historical Society meeting. She insisted they join her and Mrs. Jarvis for tea and fresh baked berry pie.

A special dessert with good company was just what

they needed. All four were nestled in comfy wicker chairs. What made it even more perfect was that the verandah of Mrs. Benson's house, overlooked the harbor.

The sunset was spectacular and bold in colors. It was just the perfect prescription for Laurel and Dale. To help them relax from such a traumatic day.

Afterward they walked back to the Inn for a much earned rest. Dale slept fitfully that night. He kept dreaming of descending those basement stairs over and over again. He had the feeling of continually looking for something, but it was not there.

Early the next morning, a call came through the Inn lines, from Ontario. It was Dale's principal. There had been a clerical mistake in the posted date for his upcoming course. It would be starting one week sooner than listed. This meant that Dale had to return immediately. He did not want to miss out on the course credits.

They decided that the shuttle to the airport would work fine. Dale could fly out of Yarmouth. It was just one hour away. It would allow Dale to leave Laurel with the car. This would save them a lot, not having to rent a second vehicle for the two weeks.

Dale was comfortable to leave Laurel alone. He expressed that his comfort levels were higher knowing Kaela and Sol could help Laurel, sort things and keep her company.

It would also mean that they would not have to cancel the roofer. He was due the following Monday. The roof had to be measured in order to purchase supplies. They would have to stop by the builders supply this afternoon to choose the shingle style and color.

Dale made a quick call to Kaela and Sol's mother. He requested assurance that they would not leave Laurel alone at the house. Laurel objected, not seeing this as necessary, but Dale did. He just had a bad feeling about the whole thing. It would have left him worried.

"Please dear, humor me. I will be unable to concentrate on my course, if I know that you are alone here."

The following morning at breakfast, Laurel decided.

Once she saw Dale off on the Yarmouth shuttle, she planned to spend the day clearing brush. She wanted to concentrate mostly around the path down to the beach and the overgrown raspberry patch.

A stop at the hardware store provided two sturdy clippers; three pairs of work gloves and a hand held brush saw.

It was a sunny and breezy day. It promised to be a good one for working outside. Not to mention the fact that it would give Laurel a much needed break, from the emotional turmoil of that mysterious house.

On her way down to Fort Point, Laurel picked up Kaela and Sol. They started right away, clearing in the front yard, working for over an hour, nonstop. Laurel selected a good spot for a bonfire. They began to pile the brush there.

Sol viewing the growing pile exclaimed, “When you are ready to burn this pile, my dad would love to come down and do it for you.”

“His two favorite things in the world to do, is to have bonfires and set off fireworks. Mom calls him her own personal pyromaniac.”

By mid morning Laurel suggested she get everyone cold drinks from the cooler. Both kids agreed, it was a good idea.

After some time, Sol realized that Laurel had not returned.

Feeling that something was wrong, both he and Kaela rushed into the house to look for her.

They found Laurel sitting at the top of the basement stairs, holding three cans of soda. She was staring down into the gloom.

Laurel seemed oblivious to their presence. Kaela called her name, this snapped Laurel out of her trance. She asked Laurel, what was wrong? Still trance like, Laurel answered, "I feel drawn to the basement. Would you and Sol mind taking a break from the yard work, to go back down with me?"

The last thing that Kaela and Sol wanted to do right away was to return to that eerie basement.

Unfortunately the strange look on Laurel's face left them with no option, but to comply with her request.

Laurel lit the lanterns and led the procession down the stairs. After hanging the lanterns on the beams, the three explorers wandered around the outer walls once more.

It was all so strange. Laurel could feel it in her bones. There had to be something more to it, something beyond the obvious.

12. Revelation

Looking around the basement, Laurel suggested, “Sol, could you sweep up a bit, while Kaela and I clear off the shelves?”

With this plan of action, Kaela returned to the kitchen to collect garbage bags. Sol went with her to claim the broom and dustpan. On returning, he started to sweep in one corner.

Kaela and Laurel went directly to the shelves. As they removed the jars of preserves, each one was held up to the lantern, to try and guess what it had been. The jars amounted to mostly a brown substance. Given the large patch outside, Laurel deducted that it had all been raspberry jam, many years ago.

Kaela held the garbage bag open for Laurel to carefully place the jars in. Clearing the shelves from bottom to top, there was one jar that Laurel could not reach. She grabbed the sides of the shelving unit and places one foot on the bottom shelf. This would give her a boost in order to reach that last jar.

Sol realized what was about to happen, but it all went so fast, he did not have a chance to call out.

The next instant there was the sound of splintering wood. Laurel, the bottom shelf and the lone jar of preserves went crashing to the concrete floor.

Sol rushed over to help. He was relieved to see Laurel move a bit. Once her head stopped spinning, she assured Sol that she was alright. Laurel had certainly fared a lot better than the bottom shelf. The burst canning jar of pickles was now spreading a faint odor of vinegar in the air.

After cleaning up the broken wood, glass and pickles, Laurel decided that the entire shelving unit was not safe. Sol had no difficulty pulling down the remaining shelves, then the left and right sides.

Then he grabbed the backing and gave a pull. The right edge seemed to move a bit, but the left edge appeared to be quite solid. He let go and went up to the kitchen to get the pry bar. Back in the basement Sol inserted the pry bar in behind the left side of the panel. He pulled with all his strength, but nothing budged.

Sol thought 'This is certainly strange. The rest of the shelving all but fell apart in my hands.' Sol unhooked a lantern from the ceiling beam, so that he could have a better look.

What Sol's eyes beheld, made him gasp and started his heart pounding. Laurel had gone up to the kitchen with an armload of broken wood. Sol called out to her, frozen on the spot.

Laurel sensed the urgency in his voice. She rushed back down the stairs to his side. Sol was speechless! He could only point to the three heavy hinges. They were neatly hidden, behind the left side of the panel.

Kaela, Sol and Laurel stood in front of the panel, silently staring. They all wanted to grab the loose side and swing it open, but did not have the nerve. Knowing that the answer to all this mystery, had to be hidden here. They were so close now, but feared the unknown.

Finally after what felt like forever, Sol gathered enough resolve to approach the panel. Placing both hands on the loose edge, he slowly slid the panel away from the wall.

Laurel lifted the lantern off the floor. All three crept silently and carefully closer. Before them lay the incredible sight that had long been hiding behind the shelf panel.

Set into a concrete frame, was a heavy metal door. Sol hit it with the side of his fist and winced. It was solid steel for sure; there was no give at all. It had a concave grip on the right side. Beside this was a shaped hole. It was obviously there for a key. They examined the entire door closely. It was clear that a key would be the only way to open it.

13. The Key Hunt

Laurel, Kaela and Sol made a thorough search of the basement. Shining the torch and feeling into every crack and crevice. They came up empty handed. Next they went up to the kitchen. Meticulously searching, into and behind everything. From there the process was repeated throughout every room in the house.

The next obvious place to search, was at the Inn. They all piled into the car for the trip to town.

A thorough search through the box was conducted. It contained the personal items that Uncle Albert had left behind. This search provided no results. All three sat on the floor, now surrounded by the contents of the box.

Laurel suddenly exclaimed, “The Home!” Quickly they rushed down the street to the seniors care home. The owner was very kind. She had no problem letting them see Uncle Albert's former room. Laurel explained, “We are missing an important key. I suspect that Uncle Albert might have hidden it here in his room.”

Thankfully the current resident was away with family

that day. She would have surely been upset to see three strangers exploring her room. They again looked in, under and behind everything, with no luck.

As they were about to leave, the dresser caught Sol's eye. He had recently read a mystery, one of his favorite series. In it, secret messages were passed on, by being taped to the back or underside of a drawer.

He felt a shiver run up his spine. He just knew that the dresser had to hold the secret. Sol started at the top, sliding each drawer fully out, in order to examine under and behind. The first three were clear, but 'Bingo' the forth one stuck. It was difficult to fully remove.

Once out, it revealed a thick packet. It was taped to the underside, near the back. Even before he tore the packet open, Sol knew. The shape and weight was right. It had to be the key to the mysterious steel door.

They thanked the owner of the residence and left. Driving back to Fort Point no one spoke. All three were lost in thought, about what might be hidden behind the door.

Foe Kaela it was the fascination and horrors of dead bodies. For Sol it was pirate treasure. It just had to be a massive stash of pirate treasure! For Laurel, after all the trauma and uncertainty, it was just too much to think about. Uncle Albert, the letter and the strange seemingly not lived in house, her mind was swirling. She was unable to clearly focus on even one idea, of what could possibly lie behind that door.

Arriving at the house, they quickly paraded through and down the basement stairs. Laurel carefully lit the lanterns. She hung one on a nail and then carried the other one over to the steel door.

Sol stood there, with laurel and Kaela on either side. He held the key, mesmerized by the key hole. He was positive that it would fit, but was afraid to try it. Finally he raised the key and slid it into the hole.

The sight of seeing it slide in easily, made Sol's heart thump. He tried to rotate the key, but it resisted moving. Sol took a deep breath, gripping the key firmly with both hands. He added pressure to the turn.

The key made a grating sound, then started to slowly rotate. It was obviously rusty, not having been opened for years. When the key completed its turn, the tumblers inside the lock gave a loud clunk, everyone gasped.

14. To The Unknown

Laurel grasped for Kaela's hand. She did not have the nerve to reach for the door handle. Sol seized the recessed handle and pulled. The door was extremely heavy. It took all of his strength to lever it open.

Once it was swung wide, Laurel lifted the lantern and peered into the opening. The glow revealed a short flight of concrete stairs, with a wooden door at the base.

As if in a spell, all three slowly walked down the stairs. Stopping at the wood door, Laurel reached out to test the door knob. She fully expected it to be solidly locked. To her shock, it was not locked. It swung open easily.

In stunned amazement, they entered a room that was finished and furnished. No bodies or pirate treasure! It contained a small kitchen area that held a little table and one chair. Near this sat an old easy chair, resting beside a small side table that held an old radio. A shelf over the radio contained several framed photos. Laurel recognized early pictures of a young Dale and his parents. Against the wall stood a bookcase. It was filled with hard cover books and piles of newspapers and magazines.

On the other side of the room sat a single bed. Nearby there was a tall wooden cupboard. It had drawers on one side and a long door that contained a mirror on the other half. The door was ajar revealing old clothing hung inside.

Looking all around herself, Laurel realized that she was seeing an almost complete living area. Laurel exclaimed, “This has to be uncle Albert's living quarters. Like everything else here, it makes no sense. Why would uncle Albert live in a sub basement, when he had a whole house above?”

They wandered around the room, looking it all over. Everyone came to a stop at the one thing that did not suggest domesticity. Another heavy wooden door. It matched the entrance door.

Sol turned to Laurel and Kaela, “Well we have come this far. No point in turning back now!” In his heart, he so hoped that Laurel would say, “Turn back.” Or it would end up being just a closet filled with junk, or clothes. But in his mind’s eye, he just knew that this door would reveal the answers to all this mystery.

Sol ever so slowly eased the door open. He held the

lantern high to light the space beyond. The glow of the lantern revealed a long flight of concrete stairs. In the limited glow of the lantern, he could just make out two landings.

In a tight group, they slowly made their way down the first flight of stairs. On the first landing, they found another wooden door. Kaela reached out to grab the doorknob. She had difficulty doing so. Her hand was shaking along with her stomach.

They dared not enter, but shone the light in. It was a large room. There was what looked like maps on the walls. Spread all around were tables, chairs, desks and filing cabinets. The floor was littered with sheets of paper.

Unable to fathom what they were seeing, all three turned and proceeded down the stairs to the next landing. The further they descended, the air became increasingly musty and damp.

The door on this landing opened to another large room. The glow of the lantern revealed a kitchen area on the left. In the center there sat a long table that was surrounded by many chairs.

On the opposite wall, stood a row of metal bunk beds.

They looked like military furnishings, with metal lockers and night stands.

In total amazement they turned back, intending to go further down the staircase. Only to realize, that directly across the landing, there was another wooden door.

Laurel opened this door and shone the lantern in. This room was similar to the one that they had just looked at. Except in this one, the furnishings looked a lot nicer. There were single beds, not bunks. It also had floor carpets and sofa chairs that formed a small living area.

What caught Laurel's eye was a large floor standing radio. On top of this sat a phonograph turntable. Strangely beside this Laurel could see a heavily draped window.

15. A View To What

It seemed incredible. On top of everything else, what was a large window doing underground? All three were drawn towards it; A window seemed so out of place. Laurel slowly drew the half rotted drapery aside. She naturally expected to see daylight flooding in. Instead there was only an eerie green glow. It looked to be way off to the left.

Sol realized that the lantern was reflecting off the glass. He took it from laurels hand and turned to set it down on the floor. Raising his line of vision from the lantern, he immediately froze. There was a man watching them from the other side of the room! Sol was speechless, he could only point. Kaela and Laurel turned to see what Sol was pointing at. Eyes wide in fear, they grabbed each other.

It took what seemed like forever, to realize that the man was not moving. Sol picked up the lantern and slowly edged forward. As he got closer, he could now see it clearer. He was looking at a life sized framed poster of a military officer.

As Laurel and Kaela joined Sol in the middle of the room, Laurel gasped and froze. She recognized the military man in the poster. It was a very real life sized image of Adolf Hitler.

The lights in Laurel's mind were for sure, now shining bright. She turned to Kaela and Sol exclaiming, "This is Uncle Albert's secret. This is the secret that he and Dale's parents took to their graves." Completely shaken, Laurel now had the resolve to finish uncovering the entire mystery.

They turned back and once again tried to look through the window. Still they could only see a black void, with an eerie glow off to the left.

There was no turning back now. They were driven to proceed down the stairs, in search of all the answers. Re tracing their steps back to the staircase, they carefully descended further. This flight of stairs seemed an unusually long way down. Reaching the bottom, they found themselves standing on another concrete floor.

Sol now holding the lantern, shone it to the right. It revealed the form of packing crates. They were stacked beyond the reach of his light.

Laurel slowly edged to the left, with Kaela and Sol in

tow. With each step in this direction, they increasingly became aware of the nearness of water. A few feet further on, all three were standing at the water's edge.

Spread out before them was a channel. It looked to be at least thirty feet wide and extremely long. It was surrounded on three sides by concrete.

A little further along, they were standing at the head of another identical channel. There was still a feeling of space beyond. They slowly crept forward expecting to find another channel.

What took form before them, in the weak glow of the lantern, stopped all three dead in their tracks. Laurel, Kaela and Sol were amazingly standing before the bow of a submarine! As if in a dream, they slowly observed it, walking along the concrete edge. As they reached the conning tower, Laurel almost screamed. The glow of Sol's lantern had revealed a faded swastika, with the insignia U-889.

When the initial shock began to wear off, something caught Sol's eye. He handed Laurel the lantern. Stepping gingerly along the edge of the concrete, Sol eased towards the stern of the submarine. This brought him to where the concrete ended. Before him, fueled by sunlight that was filtered through sea water, was the source of the eerie green glow. It looked like a pair of large doors, set below the water. One door was broken away from its top hinge, resting slightly ajar.

Suddenly the lantern in Laurel's hand gave a sputter. She knew from experience, that it was a signal of low fuel. Her nerves were shot. She didn't want to be stranded down there in the dark.

Laurel grabbed Kaela's hand and called out to Sol, to hurry back. Quickly they re traced their path up the stairs. This time not pausing at any landings, until they reached the house basement.

The lantern that had been left hanging from the basement beam was already out. The lantern in Laurel's hand went dark just as they started up the basement stairs. Thankfully daylight was streaming down, to light their way. Not stopping in the kitchen, all three kept rushing until they were once again outside in sunlight.

16. Authorities

After a while, sitting on the edge of the stoop, Sol exclaimed, "Now what?" Trying to gather her thoughts, Laurel decided, "Let's go to town and notify someone." She was in such a state; Her mind could not process clearly. Driving the distance to town, helped to at least normalize her breathing. But it did nothing to clear Laurel's thought process.

Reaching town, Laurel drove along the main street. She noticed a sign. It pointed up a side street to the left. On it was boldly posted RCMP. Laurel swung the car up that street. She was soon parked beside the detachment office.

All three rushed out of the car, through the front door and urgently burst into the waiting area. Their momentum fell flat, when a young officer ambled over to the counter and asked if she could help them.

Laurel turned, looked at Kaela and Sol, then back to the officer. She was totally unable to speak. The officer could see that Laurel looked distressed. She came around thecounter, ushering all three to a row of chairs.

Once seated, she addressed them, "Please rest and take your time. Is this an emergency? Laurel looked wide eyed at the officer. She could only shake her head. After all, where do you start? It did not fall into her life's experience to walk into a police station to confess, "I have a Nazi submarine base under my house."

When slowly some thoughts began to form in her head, Laurel looked up at the officer, "Please call someone in Ottawa." Puzzled the officer asked, "Who would you like me to call?"

Sol blurted out, "Someone in charge of spies and submarines!"

The officer's eyes widened at hearing this. Looking at the expressions on their faces, she went behind the counter. She returned shortly with three glasses of cold water. As they sipped the water she told them, "My superior will be arriving in a few minutes. He will know what to do, or who to call."

After his arrival and many questions, the Sergeant did phone Ottawa. He eventually contacted the appropriate person at National Defense. Once off the phone he asked, "Would you all feel up to going back out to Fort Point? If I can see what you are describing, it will help me when it comes to writing a full report." He wondered if it was for real, or just a tall tale, thinking, 'I hope I didn't jump the gun.'

'I will look really bad in front of my superiors, if I called Ottawa and it turns out to be a hoax.'

It was agreed. It took a few minutes to collect some high powered lanterns from his supplies. Once set, he and another officer followed Laurel's car, around the harbor to Fort Point.

As they were passing through Gunning Cove, Sol began to chuckle. Kaela asked him, "What's so funny?" Sol replied, "Just wait till we get back to school in September. Our teacher will ask us what we did on our summer vacation." With this statement, their nervous spell was broken. They all laughed together.

This time, knowing what to expect, they were able to absorb more details. They slowly led the officers down through the rooms. Everything was clearer, aided by the stronger lanterns.

The living quarters were neat, but the large office room had papers strewn all over the floor. The empty file drawers were all hanging open. Almost every chair was tipped over.

Down on the water level, the high powered lanterns lit more of what they had not seen. There were movable cranes, perched above the stacks of crated supplies. Torpedoes, neatly resting in rows, on wooden rack. Plus lots of machinery. All of this would have been used in the maintenance and repair of submarines.

17. Military Brass

The following morning and several after that, large numbers of official looking military people arrived. They came from both Halifax and Ottawa.

Dale had been snatched from his course by the RCMP. He was rushed back from Ontario via military cargo plane. He could hardly believe or fathom the wild story that Laurel had frantically told him. It was a telephone call that he would never forget.

On the surface, they observed the property being gone over with a fine tooth comb. They had found bits of metal and tools under the surface of the ground. As each piece was detected, the only way to reach it was to clear away the alders and wild brush.

Laurel chuckled at this. In the military's quest for evidence, they were doing a lot of the clearing work for her. The yard and surrounding hill down to the ocean, was fast becoming a beautiful open area.

Both Dale and Laurel assumed that the military was also combing every inch of the underground facility.

They were not allowed below ground, for several days.

A military Liaison Officer had been placed in charge of the operation. He explained that denying access was a precaution. In his words, "There are safety concerns about the stability of the torpedoes and other live ordinance that has been sitting on the damp water level for too many years. The entire area is off limits until the bomb disposal team gives the all clear."

Dale was sure about what they were not saying. That it was also about paper work. He was amazed that any of it could still be deemed sensitive, after all these years.

One question that Laurel thought of and asked several days later was, "What happened to the Royal Navy sailors back in 1945? They had motored the U-Boat out of the harbor, supposedly on its way to New York. There it was to be studied and dismantled."

Every official that Laurel asked either ignored her question, or immediately changed the subject. In the end she assumed that they either did not know, or were not allowed to say.

Almost one week passed, with a lot of coming and going. Kaela and Sol were fast becoming local celebrities, with the neighbors and their friends. A village of tents and trailers had been set up in the yard. They housed offices and equipment for security and other personnel.

As the trailers were being positioned, electrical crews installed new power lines and a temporary panel, mounted on a new pole.

This made Dale realize that they would have to bring in a totally new power source, to electrify the house. He decided to try and keep the new pole and panel in place, when the military were finished with it

Many more personnel were billeted a short hop across the harbour, at the nearby Sandy Point Naval Base. A small military floating pontoon wharf was set up on the beach below the house. Personnel were ferried daily, back and forth by launch. Laurel assumed that this was done to reduce traffic through the town, in order to try and keep a lower profile of the discovery.

As things go in a small town, it was soon buzzing with questions and gossip. Dale and Laurel kept out of sight as much as possible. Keeping a low profile helped them to avoid questions by locals.

It was also drummed into them to stay away from every aspect of the media. Things were difficult and strained enough. The warnings of being charged with a breach of security would only complicate the situation.

It was during this week that the Editor of the Local newspaper, The Coast Guard, rebelled at being refused access. He called his friend, the editor of the Halifax Herald. He urged him to send a reporter down, in hopes of getting an exclusive story.

This call let to Jeff Hendricks arrival at the Inn, to interview Laurel and Dale. Assuming that he would now get a scoop, that he could rush to press.

Jeff had no sooner taken a sip of his coffee, when they were immediately interrupted by an RCMP Officer. He was accompanied by a Military Official and a commissioned recording clerk.

The officer addressed Jeff directly, "We will not at this time go into how you were tipped off about what is happening here. It will be decided later if charges will be laid."

"I have however been authorized to allow this interview to take place. As long as you swear an oath and agree to sign a statement. By the terms of this, you will not be allowed to publish a word of this story, until the Navy gives you official clearance to do so."

He assured Jeff, "I have it on authority that the exclusive will remain yours. It will not be long, before you are released to publish."

Kaela and Sol spent part of every day, watching the military activities with Laurel and Dale. On the fifth day, a small military barge arrived. Mounted on its deck was a lifting crane. It was moored over the entrance, to what they now learned, was called, 'A U-Boat Pen'. Divers with welding gear could be seen going in and out of the water, obviously to repair the broken door. Dale made a mental note to observe this activity closely. There was no way that he would allow even the idea of removing the U-Boat from their property.

It had been discovered by Laurel and the kids. Not by the military. As far as he was concerned, the rules of finders' keepers, on top of possession being nine tenths of the law, applied here.

At the same time large trucks arrived. They were soon being loaded. Some of the crates had German markings, but others were new. Everything had to be laboriously moved up the staircase and through the house. Larger crates or torpedoes would have to wait for a cargo sub, if they even existed. Baring this, they would all have to be left behind. This suited Dale just fine. As long as the explosives were removed, he liked the idea of having the torpedo casings left near 'His U-Boat'.

Observing the loading of unknown equipment, Dale confronted the Commander in charge. He informed him, “All of this is our private property. It has been for many decades.” He insisted, “If the Navy wishes to remove anything, they had better have Laurel and myself involved. If not, I intend to disregard the Navy's forced restrictions. I will immediately go public with what we found under our house.”

A few heated phone calls and a day later, Laurel and Dale met with a civil servant. He was introduced as being from National Security. Mr. Forje’ looked frazzled, as if he had been beamed in, right from his desk in Ottawa.

Being a true bureaucrat, he rambled on and on. In the end they came to one simple conclusion. ‘As there is no longer an official war on. the War Measures Act and or security acts could not be used to keep them in line.’

However he was authorized by Ottawa, to sit down with them, to work out a mutually agreed on plan. Hearing this, confirmed Dales belief in ownership.

They went along with this, except demanding one

condition. That he meet with them and a lawyer of their choice, to formalize and sign the agreement.

Mr. Forje' started to object to this request, but Dale cut in. "I assure you that having our lawyer present, is not to add to the negotiations. But rather to assist us in being clear, about everything that we are agreeing to.

Mr. Forje' conceded, "As long as all parties involved will swear an oath of silence. This will hold in force until the Military investigation is completed." Dale added, "To this site." Forje' reluctantly agreed.

Laurel and Dale's next mission was to go to town and see Mr. Anderson. He had handled Uncle Albert's will as well as the property transfer. They had to convince him the importance of freeing up a good part of the next day, to be at Fort Point. It was difficult, because they were not allowed to give him any real details. Not until he was at the site and sworn in.

After arranging to pick Mr. Anderson up, the following morning, they decided to not return to Fort Point that day. Opting to take a drive. They meandered along the shore route out of town.

The scenery was beautiful. They took a long walk on the windswept and deserted Roseway Beach. It was sparkling, with pounding surf and clear white sand. Laurel and Dale realized that taking a break, was a good idea. The tension of the last week, had them both wound tight.

As Dale and Laurel began to relax, they nearly collapsed from pent up exhaustion. They returned to the Inn early in the evening and went to bed. Accepting, that their lives will be quite different, from now on.

After all, many people have a summer home on the ocean. But not boasting a subterranean WWII German U-Boat base. If that, in itself, was not unique enough. They were also the owners of an actual operational U-Boat.

18. Negotiations

The following morning, after an early breakfast Laurel and Dale set off. They picked up Mr. Anderson at his office and drove directly to Fort Point. There they found Kaela and Sol anxiously waiting.

Mr. Forje' had set up a table with chairs in the living room. There were also several other tables lined up against one wall. They held computers, phones and piles of papers.

A recording clerk appeared, with a tray containing coffee and soft drinks. Once he served these, he immediately produced a bible. One by one they were all sworn to secrecy. Dale was not pleased to comply. But under the circumstances, he did not feel that they had a great deal of leverage or authority.

Mr. Forje' took nearly an hour, to fill Mr. Anderson in. He also brought them all up to date as to what had been happening below ground. Now everyone could view the site, knowing everything that had transpired in the past week.

Dale wished that he had a video camera, to capture the look on Mr. Anderson's face. His mouth was agape as he heard the incredible story for the first time.

Finally the briefing was finished and papers signed. Dale insisted that they all be taken on a complete tour. Other than the house and basement, he had not as yet seen what lay below. Plus Mr. Anderson had not seen it at all.

Dale announced, “A tour will help everyone understand everything that we discussed and agreed on today.” What he really meant was. They were all dying of curiosity as to what had been found and done down there. It was a complete unknown, because of being barred entry.

Mr. Forje’ was reluctant at first. After a call to his superior in Ottawa, he agreed. They paraded to the basement, where everyone examined the steel door. Then down the stairs to uncle Albert’s underground dwelling.

All was fairly neat, although the room was now totally dust free. Laurel could tell that it showed signs of being thoroughly gone through.

Mr. Forje’ explained, “This area proved to hold only Albert's personal possessions. Other than providing a land access route, from above ground. This area had no military relevance to the complex below."

Dale was amazed to see for the first time, where his uncle Albert had actually lived.

19. The Grand Tour

Laurel, Kaela and Sol, no longer treading in fear, did not realize at first that the lights were all working. Laurel was now seeing clearly, all the way down the flight of stairs to the first landing. She commented on her realization. Mr. Forje' stated, "The generators were left in perfect condition."

"They needed only servicing, wiring checks and fresh diesel fuel, to get everything up and running."

The office, or as Mr. Forje' called it, "The Operations Room", was as before. But it had understandably been stripped clean of every scrap of paper. The lower living quarters also looked neater than Laurel remembered.

On entering the Officers Quarters, Laurel, Kaela and Sol were immediately drawn to that mysterious window. It was now glowing with bright light. It made perfect sense. From this vantage point, they could observe the entire docking area. Plus all the activity that was now going on, down there.

The boat level had seen most of the action. It was so much larger than it had seemed in the dark. There were military personnel everywhere. Some were dismantling torpedoes. Others were crating machinery for shipment.

Dale announced again, "All of this is probably ours. I question the legality of the Military in removing any part of it." He looked to Mr. Anderson in support of his claim.

Mr. Anderson stated, "To date my realty experience has never had to deal with subterranean military installations, nor the ownership of submarines.

He suggested, "While I look into this, we should at least be provided with a signed inventory, of anything being removed from the premises."

Mr. Forje', while visibly not happy, agreed. Like a tour group, they walked around the docking areas. Everyone, taking in the activity. They were fascinated, examining the interesting array of munitions, supplies and machinery.

When finally they approached the U-Boat, Laurel, Kaela and Sol were totally amazed. Now that it was completely illuminated, they could see in total, just how large it is. A gangplank had been installed. It allowed access to the U-Boat deck, just forward of the conning tower.

Suddenly an idea flashed in Dale's mind. He stepped ahead of everyone, and stood for the first time on the U-Boat's metal hull grating. He smartly turned facing the tour group. They were all gathered on the concrete, about to cross the gangplank. Before they could move towards him, he made an announcement, "Good morning. My name is Captain Dale Peters. I would like to invite you all aboard my U-Boat, for a personal tour." In making this statement, Dale loudly emphasized the words, "MY U-BOAT". Everyone chuckled, with the exception of Mr. Forje'. He had a bleak expression on his face.

They all filed across the gangplank. Then one by one, proceeded up the ladder, to the top of the conning tower. In single file, they started to climb down through the main hatch.

Laurel hesitated, asking Mr. Forje', "Did you find any bodies in the U-Boat?" In all the excitement, neither she nor Dale had thought about bodies. Probably because they had not yet seen any sign of human presence.

Mr. Forje' assured Laurel, "There have been no bodies found, nor even any sign that there has even been any." With a sigh of relief, Laurel continued her climb down to the control room.

Everyone was awed at the sight of all the machinery, wheels and dials. Dale closely examined the periscope shaft. He shivered at the thought of raising it above the surface of the sea, to scan for enemy ships.

Space was very tight, in the central command area. It did not get larger as they squeezed through each watertight hatch.

In the forward and aft ends, there was a lot more space. This was due to the empty torpedo racks. Sol asked, "Did the military take all of the torpedoes out of the boat?" Mr. Forje' answered, "The U-Boat was found empty of ordinance. It had been de-ammunitioned at the Shelburne pier, back in the spring of 1945. That was just before its reported ill-fated sailing to New York.

Dale was speechless, actually being aboard a real U-Boat. After all the war movies he had watched as a boy. Like many other Post-War children, his fantasy had been to serve as the heroic Captain of a submarine.

20. The Future

It took two more weeks for the military to complete their investigation of the U-Boat and the base. Now they were no longer banned from below. Dale, Laurel, Kaela and Sol spent many hours observing the action.

Dale realized that if they wanted to continue having access to the entire complex, he would have to install a much larger than usual electrical panel in the house. Once connected to the grid, they could at least run the lighting below ground. If it was ever needed to run the cranes or other equipment, Dale hoped that the generators could be brought on line for a short while, to handle the strain.

In the midst of all the activity one afternoon, they had a visitor. A Mrs. Wendy Burry arrived at Fort Point. She represented the Shelburne Town Tourist Association. She emphasized, "The Association is most interested in having you open the house and its underground secrets to the public."

"This would make an excellent tourist attraction. You could charge admission to offset the costs of the operation."

"I have worked with the Tourism Grant people many times. I hear from the bulk oil dealer that you are running on diesel. There would be grants available to connect to the grid. It would just mean a commitment to be open to the public for several seasons."

"The spin-off for the local restaurants and accommodation operators would be ever so helpful.'

"We can even help with planning and managing the facility. Not to mention the grants available to help hire tour guides and maintenance staff."

Wendy Burry's visit confirmed Dale and Laurel's belief. Their secret was now public knowledge in the town. It had even spread up and down the shore to neighboring towns and villages. Certainly every resident that lived on the harbor was aware of all the activity, in detail.

Laurel and Dale discussed the proposal. They let Mrs. Burry know a few days later, "We will probably end up doing as you suggested. But at this point, we are committed to waiting for the Military to give us total clearance. Then we need some time to rest and get a grip on it all. With everything you have suggested, I am sure that it would be next season before we could envision opening to the public."

Wendy agreed, "Yes, the tourism infrastructure grants have already been awarded for this year. The sooner we bring the provincial people in, the better. They can pre approve plans for next season. That way, having their guarantees, infrastructure work such as electricity and brochure planning can be done well ahead of the season.

The next few summers proved to be busy ones. With daily tours running, for the base and the U-boat.

Kaela and Sol worked themselves into full time summer employment, for the duration of their school years. They were a great hit with all of the tourists. Daily greeting everyone, with their happy personalities. The fact that they had been involved from the beginning of the discovery, made them resident celebrities.

After all, how many children can claim to have discovered a secret subterranean U-Boat pen, complete with its own U-Boat!

21. Mysteries Revealed

The complex turned out to be a roaring success. Tourism hired a designer to re do the inside of the house to reflect the war time period. The wall coverings and furniture were all old and basic. There was nothing out of place that a bachelor of the time who lived alone, would not have. There was an infrastructure need, to provide washroom facilities for the tourists. Being unable to set up the house for their use, Dale and Laurel opted to place a tiny home, between the barn and the path to the beach.

It was a warm breezy day in late July. This was the third full summer that Kaela and Sol were busy, along with several other guides. Ushering tourists through the complex took time.

Each party had to be accompanied by a guide for safety, down through the subterranean staircases and rooms. Also around the docking areas and through the U-Boat.

The main hatch was roped off to the public. A through path was devised, using the forward and aft hatches as an in and an out. With double gangplanks in place, the flow moved along smoothly.

That day the attendant on duty at the gate house was Kimberly, Kaela and Sol's mother. She had taken over managing the staffing and location needs from day one. This enabled Laurel and Dale to continue living in Ontario for the school year.

Just after lunch that day, Kimberly called over the portable pagers, “Would Kaela or Sol please come to the ticket office as soon as you are free.” Kaela was just half way through touring her group. Sol had just finished up his.

When Sol arrived at the office, he found an elderly couple waiting there. Kimberly was keeping them company. She made the introductions, “Sol this is Guntram and Alina Hiltraud. They requested that either you or Kaela be their guide.”

To Kimberly and Sol's surprise, Mr. Hiltraud explained, “I was a member of the German crew who hijacked the U-889. We stole it away from the Canadian Navy and then hid it in this secret base.”

Sol was immediately bursting with questions, having thought about it for more than three years. He kept trying to reason it all out, from every angle. He knew for sure that Uncle Albert could not have created all of this on his own.

He asked his mom to call up to the house for Laurel and Dale, to have them join the group. There was no problem reaching Kaela. He could catch her as she brought her current group back to the surface.

Sol led Mr. and Mrs. Hiltraud down to the basement, through Uncle Albert's living quarters, then on down to the officers' quarters. He held back the guide ropes so that they could all gather there and have places to sit. Sol was bursting with curiosity, to hear Mr. Hiltraud's story.

After nearly fifteen minutes, everyone was in attendance. Mr. Hiltraud began to tell his tale, of incredible events.

"Just before the war, I was a junior member of an entire U-Boat crew. We were sent to work in Halifax. We posed as clerks and other assorted staff, attached to the German Embassy."

"When it was imminent that Canada would shortly enter the war, our orders sent us to ground. One by one so not to be noticed, we took the train down the shore. We got off at various stops, above and below Fort Point. Luckily we were all able to relocate here, just before travel restrictions were enforced."

Once off the train, we made our way discreetly to Albert Peters home. There we were put to work setting up the base and accommodations below ground."

The entire complex had been secretly built. It took advantage of a natural cave system. Albert had discovered it, when he tried to dig a deep water well, in his basement."

He contacted the German Embassy in Halifax about his discovery. They had a military engineer come down to explore and survey the caves. From there they took over the entire operation."

"Construction prisoner crews, from Germany, along with large amounts of stores and equipment were quickly shipped in. It was done by using freighter U-Boats."

"The first phase of the construction was to complete the entrances to the caves."

"Both from above ground, but most importantly, from below the water level."

"It was all moved into the cavern, before Canada officially joined the hostilities. Our supply line ceased, once the harbour was sealed off by the anti submarine nets."

"We had to finish the installation work and live off the existing stores for the duration. The only added supplies were the fruit and vegetables from Albert's gardens. Plus eggs and chickens from his barn."

"If Albert had been, at all social. Any visitors would have marveled at his large well kept vegetable garden. They would also have wondered what he was doing with all that produce."

"In true fact, we sailors tended the gardens. We did the tilling and weeding by moonlight. It ensured that no one observed strangers working during the daylight hours."

All this had to be carefully orchestrated. Because of rationing, it would have drawn attention to Albert. As a lone male, it would bring on suspicion if he tried to purchase large amounts of food stuffs."

"As the truce, or German capitulation neared. We had thought that it all would end, without us being called on to actually perform as sailors."

"In one way that was disappointing. After all, we were well trained U-Boat mariners. On the other hand we were grateful. Listening to the war time broadcasts on the radio, we soon came to the sad realization. Few of our U-Boat mariner friends would be around to greet us, after it was all over. The daily reports of U-Boat sinkings saddened us.

22. Final Answers

Mr. Hiltraud continued his story, "Just three days after our government capitulated, ending the war. We received our first official orders."

"We were told that a new U-Boat had surrendered just off the nearby coast. It was reported as being escorted into this harbour. A British sub crew, were on their way from England, via corvette. Once they landed in Halifax, they were to proceed here and take possession of the U-Boat. Their orders were to navigate it to New York."

"Our communication stated that on arrival in Halifax, the sailors would be given one nights leave. Then they were expected to take the once daily train down the shore to here."

"The embassy in Halifax set up a watch. They had English speaking staff traveling back and forth, keeping an eye on the Naval Base gates."

"In time, they spotted the British sailors leaving the base, to head for the cities entertainment."

"They followed them and notified the embassy. Special

agents dressed as Canadian Navy, met up with the British sub crew in bars."

"Under the guise of celebrating the Allied victory, they made sure that the British crew all ended up drunk and out cold. They were dumped in different hotel rooms around the downtown area. Separating them was all planned to slow down their re grouping."

Late the following afternoon, the southbound train made one of its last stops in the port of Liverpool, just up the shore from Shelburne. Ten Royal Navy sailors boarded the train with tickets for the short run to town.

"Arriving at Shelburne station, we marched in formation, down the hill to Main Street."

"Then we turned south, heading for the government wharf."

"Few vehicles passed us. Gasoline rationing was still in effect. No one paid any attention. The townspeople were conditioned to seeing sailors in many allied uniforms marching about. After five years of this, few military would stand out."

"Arriving at the security gates, at the government wharf, we reported to the military police guard in charge. He had been informed that we were expected."

"Our captain did all of the talking. He had been schooled in England. He could easily pull off a polished British accent."

"The gate sentry instructed the MP on duty to escort us to the end of the pier. We then boarded the U-889. As per our orders, we immediately went to work. We did a standard pre sailing check of all the controls and systems."

"Shortly, a senior officer from the local base arrived. He handed over the charts needed to motor the U-Boat to the Brooklyn Navy Yard, in New York Harbour. He also gave us special codes to assure recognition and safety. Once formalities were completed, our engineer fired up the U-Boats engines and we cast off."

Several fishing boats and a small coast guard cutter escorted us to the harbour entrance channel."

"Our captain did not want to keep witnesses around any longer than necessary. Our nerves were running tight. If we were discovered to be imposters, it would not go well."

"As soon as our boat cleared the harbour mouth, we reached deep water. We signaled farewell and submerged."

The entire assembly, but especially Sol and Dale listened in rapture, as Mr. Hiltraud continued with his adventurous tale.

"Being the navigator, I had the charts and sailing orders from the Canadian Navy. They had us crossing the Bay Of Fundy, then following the New England coast to Boston. From there we were to pass through the channels into New York Harbour."

"Our charts placed the Naval Yard as being in the Wallabout Channel, on the Brooklyn side of the East River."

Mr. Hiltraud related, "We lay submerged off the mouth of this harbour for the balance of that day."

"When darkness fell, our Captain did a quick scan of the harbour entrance with the attack scope. He had to make sure that there was no nearby marine traffic."

"He then turned the scope over to me. At slowest speed I navigated the boat back into the harbour. I had to operate the scope at just a barely elevated level. To accomplish this I had to lie on my belly."

"Every inch of elevation enhanced the risk of a fisherman or casual observer spotting the scope."

"The flow tide and our electric motors, helped lessen

any chance of detection. Once through the channel entrance, we drifted past the now opened and unmanned anti submarine nets. Our captain brought the boat up to as shallow a depth as possible, without allowing the conning tower to breach the surface."

We kept running at slowest speed, totally on battery power. There was no need to take the risk of deploying the snorkel. We had just enough air left to complete the passage."

"We would have needed outside air from the snorkel, to run the generators, or any other pumps and machinery. But that would cause noise. The batteries were low, but the captain was sure that we could reach our destination."

"Once clear of the nets, I swung to Port. I navigated towards Fort Point. Unlike usual operations, I had the harbour chart on the floor with me. I kept constant station with the attack scope. Because we were moving at such slow speed, we did not leave a visible wake. I was terrified that I might veer ever so slightly off course and cause the boat to run aground. That would have meant capture and the end of the operation."

"Albert lit an oil lamp in the upper and lower windows of his house. This gave me a clear point of reference to navigate towards. The U-Boat pen had been darkened and the doors left open."

"Albert was waiting in the dark, by the wheels that controlled the doors. As soon as he was aware that our boat was fully inside, he hauled on the wheels and drew the steel doors closed."

"Hearing the doors clang shut, our captain surfaced the boat and called for the hatch to be opened. As soon as Albert saw the boat surface, he threw on one set of overhead lights."

"The captain took the conning tower. With the way lighted he easily maneuvered our boat into the furthest channcl mooring."

Hiltraud went on, "When all was secured and stored on the water level, we moved up to the operations and living levels."

"We helped Albert quickly sort through the paper work. We burnt anything that we thought might be important. Once these tasks were complete, following orders we started to evacuate."

"Now that hostilities were ceased, train tickets to Halifax were no longer scrutinized. They could be singularly purchased at will."

"Every three or four days, now in civilian clothing, one crew would catch the northbound train. We stared from nearby village stops, either Port Saxon or Gunning Cove and proceeded to Halifax."

"We only needed to make our way to the German Embassy. It was easy to approach the embassy. One by one we joined the lineups of Canadians. They were all trying to find news of European relatives, who had been caught up in the hostilities."

"On reaching the head of the line, we knew to ask for a pre arranged name, saying that person was a cousin, who lived in Berlin."

"This alerted the official at the desk that another submariner had arrived, seeking concealment."

"Once secure in the embassy, it was just a matter of time, before we could one by one be added to the roster of a freighter heading home."

23. Navy Embarrassment

The day after the German crew hijacked the U-889 and successfully sailed it away, the Halifax train rolled into town on schedule. The Royal Navy crew, much worse for wear, tumbled off onto the platform. In no smart order they made their way to the Government wharf. A surprised sentry stopped them at the gate when they presented their papers. Their Captain stated that they were reporting for duty to take command of the U-Boat, to sail it as ordered to New York.

The sentry, immediately called his superior. In short order he arrive with two car loads of military police. The crew were arrested and whisked away to the nearby naval base headquarters. It took several hours and many communications, before their identities were verified.

An investigation was immediately set into motion. Heads would roll if they could not determine who sailed the U-Boat away, and more so. How many levels of security failed to verify their identity and formal orders? No sign of the U-Boat or its crew were ever found or seen again.

To cover up the embarrassment to the navy, an official document was released to the press. It stated that a military investigation had been convened, into the loss of the U-889.

A few days later, preliminary findings were released stating, "Either due to bad weather, mechanical failure or inexperienced crew. The U-889 was officially listed as 'Lost At Sea'.

Finally, the last piece of the puzzle, to solve the mystery, of Uncle Albert's death's secret.

The End

Other books by Nino Balistreri soon to be in print:

Watch for two new adventure mysteries involving famous pirates and Spanish galleons:

Danger Cave: A Family Adventure. Follow the adventures of a young boy and his sister on the rugged coast of Nova Scotia in "DANGER CAVE."

Anchorage of Gold. Then explore the exciting secrets of the Florida Keys, with a nine year old boy and his father in "ANCHORAGE of GOLD."

About the Author

The author was born in Barrie, Ontario and spent his teenage years in Chicago and North Bay, Ontario. He moved to Toronto where he spent ten years studying and working, particularly in social work. Then it was on to Ottawa where he spent nine years working in chronic care and rehab. In the early 1990's, he moved to Nova Scotia where he managed the office for an arts center and an MD therapist. Around that time, he started writing seriously and has been doing so ever since.

16594570R00068

Made in the USA
Middletown, DE
24 November 2018